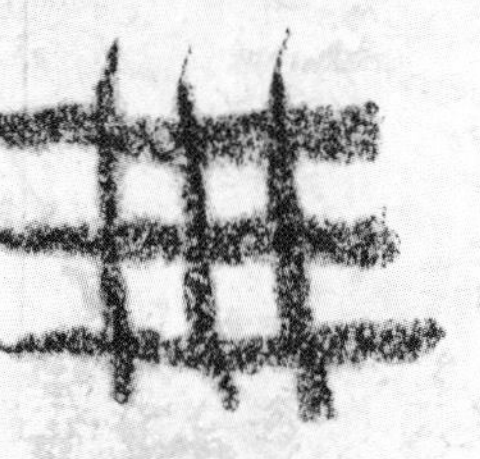

JAIL

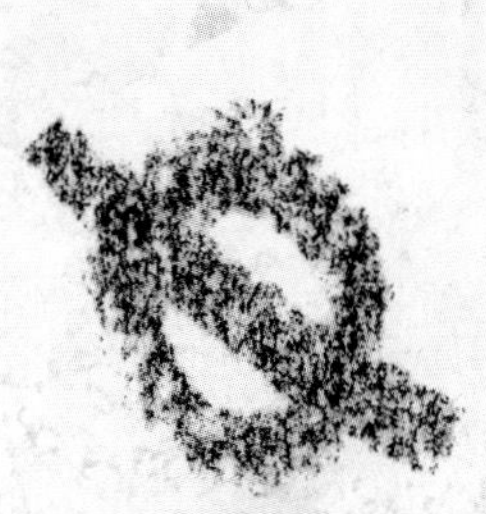

GOOD ROAD
TO FOLLOW

CATCH TRAIN
HERE

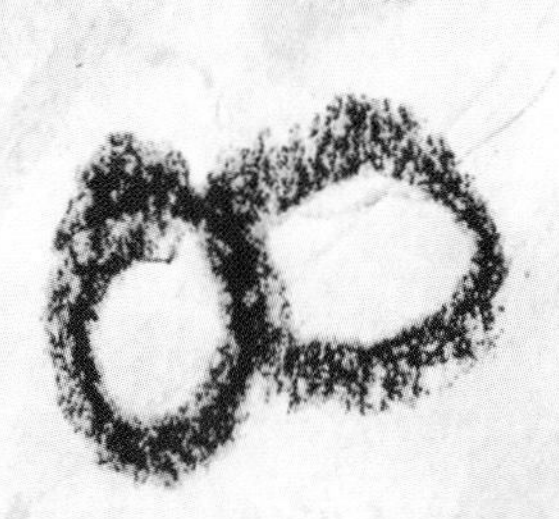

DON'T GIVE UP

KIND LADY

The CHRISTMAS PROMISE

Susan Bartoletti

ILLUSTRATED BY

David Christiana

The
BLUE SKY PRESS
An Imprint of Scholastic Inc.
New York

AUTHOR'S NOTE

When the stock market crashed and the banks closed in 1929, the United States experienced the worst economic crisis in its history. Millions of people lost their jobs and their life savings. For them, the Great Depression became a time of bread lines, soup kitchens, missions, and no work.

As the Depression deepened during the 1930s, it's estimated that over a million men, women, and children became wanderers known as hoboes. Although it was illegal and dangerous, they hopped trains and rode the rails throughout the United States and Canada. Some were seeking adventure, but most were desperate for work and a place to live.

Hoboes developed a unique communication system. Wherever they ate, slept, or passed through, they drew chalked figures on bridges, sidewalks, street curbs, or picket fences. These hobo signs let other hoboes know where to camp, beg, get help, or be aware of possible danger. The drawings also marked the homes where a hobo could find a meal, shelter, or small jobs. Different sources assign different shapes and meanings to some of these hobo signs.

THE BLUE SKY PRESS

Library of Congress catalog card number: 00-067993
ISBN 0-590-98451-9
10 9 8 7 6 5 4 3 2 1 01 02 03 04 05
Printed in Singapore 46
First printing, November 2001
Designed by Kathleen Westray

For my brother Jeff,

who always finds someplace good—S. B.

For Bonnie—D. C.

One autumn night
after Poppa's job and
his money ran out,
we packed our belongings
in bundles and followed
Main Street all the way
to the rail yard.

There a railroad bull stood guard.
When his back was turned,
we sneaked into
an open boxcar.

Soon we were riding free on the redball. "Woo-oo-o," the train called, high and thin, and its wheels clattered beneath us.

Poppa tucked my braids into my cap and told me not to worry. "We'll find someplace else that's good, Girl."

I squeezed Poppa's hand. Poppa always kept his promises.

To town after town we rode the rail, always looking for someplace good.

But town after town had the same signs. "No work." "No work." Everywhere.

Some nights Poppa found hobo signs chalked beneath railroad bridges. He taught me what they meant.

We kindled fires and roasted potatoes while freight trains rattled overhead.

Other nights we followed signs to hobo jungles, where hoboes shared mulligan stew with us. We drank coffee from soup cans and listened to stories about mean dogs and hobo kings.

Before long, the trees dropped their leaves, and it turned so cold that our breath froze in the air. To keep warm, we stuffed folded newspapers inside our coats and wrapped our shoes with tape.

Worry wrinkled Poppa's forehead as he warmed my hands in his. "You okay?" he asked.

"I'm okay," I told him. But I was worried, too—would Poppa find a place for us to live?

And that's not all I worried about. I was starting to see signs of Christmas everywhere. Santa Clauses jingled bells at street corners, and store windows showed off tiny china tea sets and dolls in pretty dresses.

"Poppa," I asked, "do hoboes have Christmas?"

He took a long time to
answer. "Yes," he said,
not looking at me.
"They figure out
a way."

Soon it grew too cold to sleep beneath railroad bridges and in hobo jungles, so we stayed in crowded missions where they fed us cold tomatoes, boiled potatoes, and muggy bread. We tied our shoes around our wrists so nobody could trade during the night.

The mission ladies taught me to pray. “Ask and ye shall receive,” they told me. “For even the sparrow finds a home and the swallow a nest.”

Night after night I prayed for someplace good.

A few weeks before Christmas,
Poppa and I jumped from a boxcar
as it slowed near a switchman's shanty.
"Hold it!" said a voice that made me shiver.
We raised our hands over our heads,
and the railroad bull marched
us to jail for trespassing.

Even the jail was decorated for Christmas. The sheriff wore a big silver star. His wife poured extra milk in my soup can and watched me with sorry eyes.

On my hand, Poppa drew two circles, one touching the other. In hobo it meant, "Don't give up."

The next morning, daylight spilled through a dirty window. The sheriff and his wife whispered back and forth with Poppa. I heard words like "school" and "proper clothing."

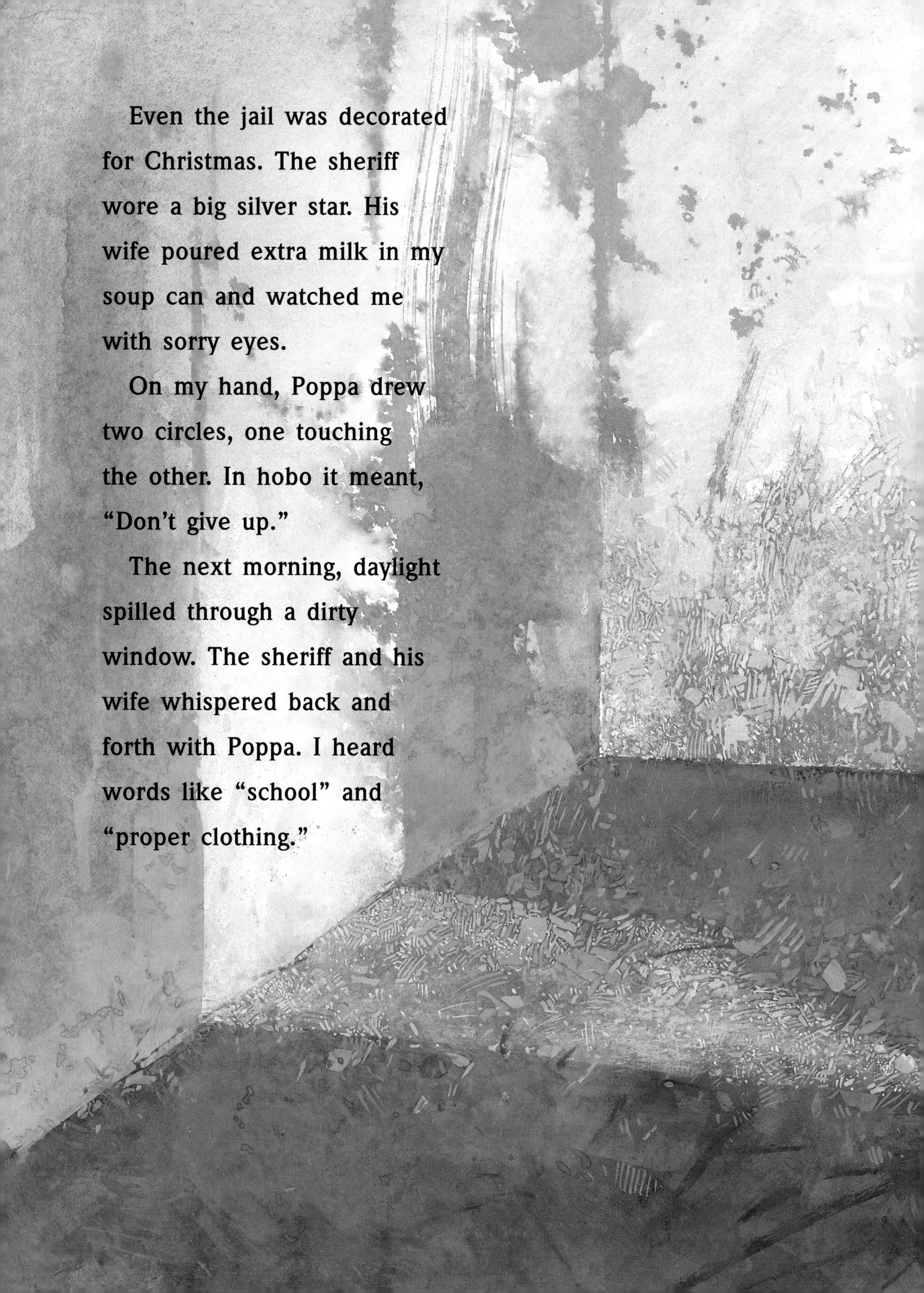

The sheriff let Poppa shave. My fingers shook as I tightened the buttons on our coats and patched a tear in Poppa's pants.

But at last we were free.
As we walked, Poppa held my hand,
not saying a word.

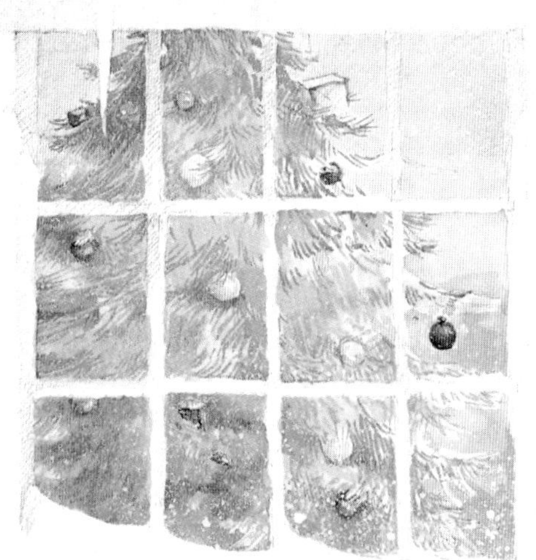

We stopped at a white clapboard house. Candles shined in the windows, and a fat tree flickered like the brightest star in the front room.

"One twenty-three Weatherby Lane," Poppa said softly.

A hobo sign was scratched on the curb. "Look, Poppa," I said. "It says 'kind lady.'"

Poppa clutched his hat and rapped twice on the back door. A wide woman with a baby on her hip answered. The baby smiled and buried his face in the woman's apron. Another small face peeked out from behind her skirt.

The kitchen smelled warm and sugary like cookies. A cookstove gleamed in one corner. Real cups with handles were stacked by the sink.

Poppa nudged me gently. "Wait outside while we talk."

I sat on the steps, wishing I could taste that kitchen a little longer. I crossed my fingers. Maybe this was the place for Poppa and me. I imagined Christmas stockings and cups of hot chocolate.

Soon Poppa was kneeling beside me. “Girl,” he said slowly. “This is someplace good for you. Especially now, with Christmas so near.”

I uncrossed my fingers. “But Poppa, what about you?”

"I'll be back as soon as I find work."
He drew two circles on my palm
and kissed my hand. "I promise."
And then he was gone.
I tried not to cry.
The woman put her arm around me.
"Let it all out," she said.

Poppa was right. One twenty-three Weatherby Lane was a good place, where nobody traded shoes during the night, and I drank hot chocolate in real cups, and I had my own stocking hanging at the fireplace.

But all those good things didn't stop me from missing Poppa. Whenever I heard the train whistle, high and thin, I thought about Poppa, riding free on the redball.

"Find someplace good. Come back for me," I prayed.

And before the first
Christmas star
came out,
he did.

FOOD FOR WORK

DANGEROUS NEIGHBORHOOD

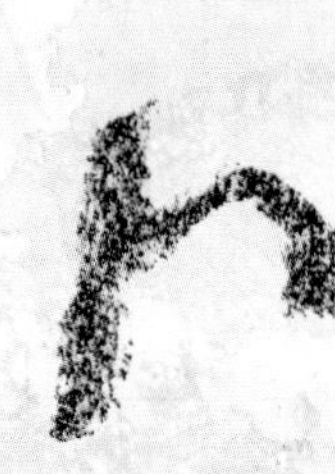

CARE HERE IF YOU ARE SICK

DON'T GO THIS WAY

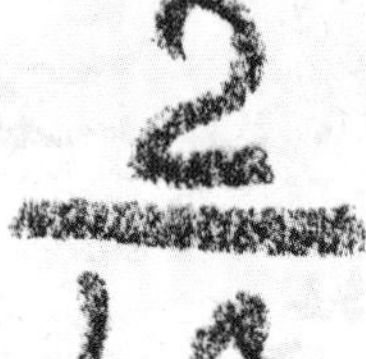

THIEVES AROUND